Illustrated by
Russell Julian

Written by
Rachel Elliot

This edition published by
Parragon Books Ltd in 2013
and distributed by

Parragon Inc.
440 Park Avenue South,
13th Floor
New York, NY 10016
www.parragon.com

Designed by Kathryn Davies
Edited by Michael Diggle
Production by Jonathan Wakeham

ISBN 978-1-4723-2908-0

Printed in China

What should I wear, Huggle Buggle Bear?

PaRRagon

Bath • New York • Singapore • Hong Kong • Cologne • Delhi
Melbourne • Amsterdam • Johannesburg • Shenzhen

Get set, Huggle Buggle,
Let's all play outside.
We'll run and we'll jump,
We'll swing and we'll slide.

Come on, Huggle Buggle,
Let's get dressed and go!
First underwear, then socks—
Where are they? Oh, no!

I've checked in the laundry
And looked in the drawer.
But there's only one sock
Lying here on the floor.

Lost! Gone!
Where could it be?
I wish Huggle Buggle
Could find it for me.

Silly Rubadub Duck—
You can't wear that.
It's my missing odd sock,
Not a funny duck's hat!

Thanks, Huggle Buggle!
You're the best-ever bear.
But I'm still not quite ready—
What else should I wear?

What if it's cold
When I whiz down the slide?
I need to be warm
To go playing outside.

I'll wear my green pants—
My favorite pair.

But where's my red sweater?
It was over there.

I must find my sweater
Before I can play.
It was hanging up—
Someone took it away!

Lost! Gone!
Where could it be?
I wish Huggle Buggle
Could find it for me.

What a surprise!
It's my friend Ellie Nellie.
My sweater's an apron
Tied around her soft belly!

Thanks, Huggle Buggle!
You're the best-ever bear.
But I'm still not quite ready—
What else should I wear?

What if it rains
When I'm swinging up high?
I want to wear something
To keep myself dry.

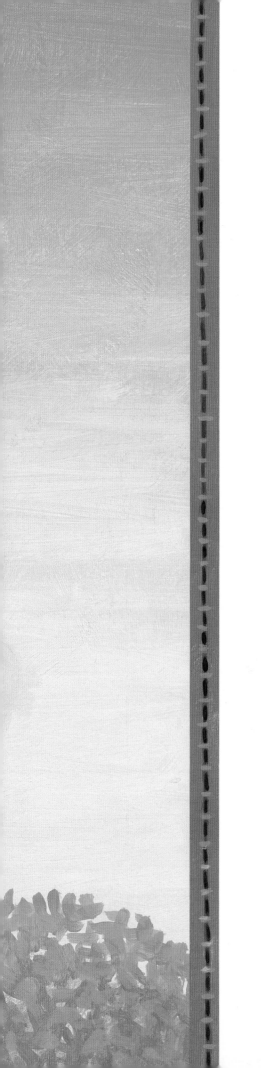

I'll put on my boots,
While I sit on this stair ...

Now, where is my coat?
Oh no, it's not there!

My coat belongs here,
On its own special hook.
It has to be found,
But where should I look?

Lost! Gone!
Where could it be?
I wish Huggle Buggle
Could find it for me.

My friend Woolly Lamb
Has borrowed my coat.
It's the wavy blue sea
Underneath his toy boat!

Thanks, Huggle Buggle!
You're the best-ever bear.
But I'm still not quite ready—
What else should I wear?

What if the wind
Blows the leaves on the ground?
I could wrap up tight
Before running around.

I'll pull on my gloves,
My snuggly hat, too ...

But where is my scarf?
Oh, what should I do?

It must be here somewhere—
It's my red and white one!
I saw it just yesterday—
Where has it gone?

Lost! Vanished!
Where could it be?
I wish Huggle Buggle
Could find it for me.

My scarf is a jump rope—
That's very funny!
But who is holding it?
Babbity Bunny!

Okay, Huggle Buggle,
What now? Do you know?
If everyone's ready,
It's playtime—LET'S GO!

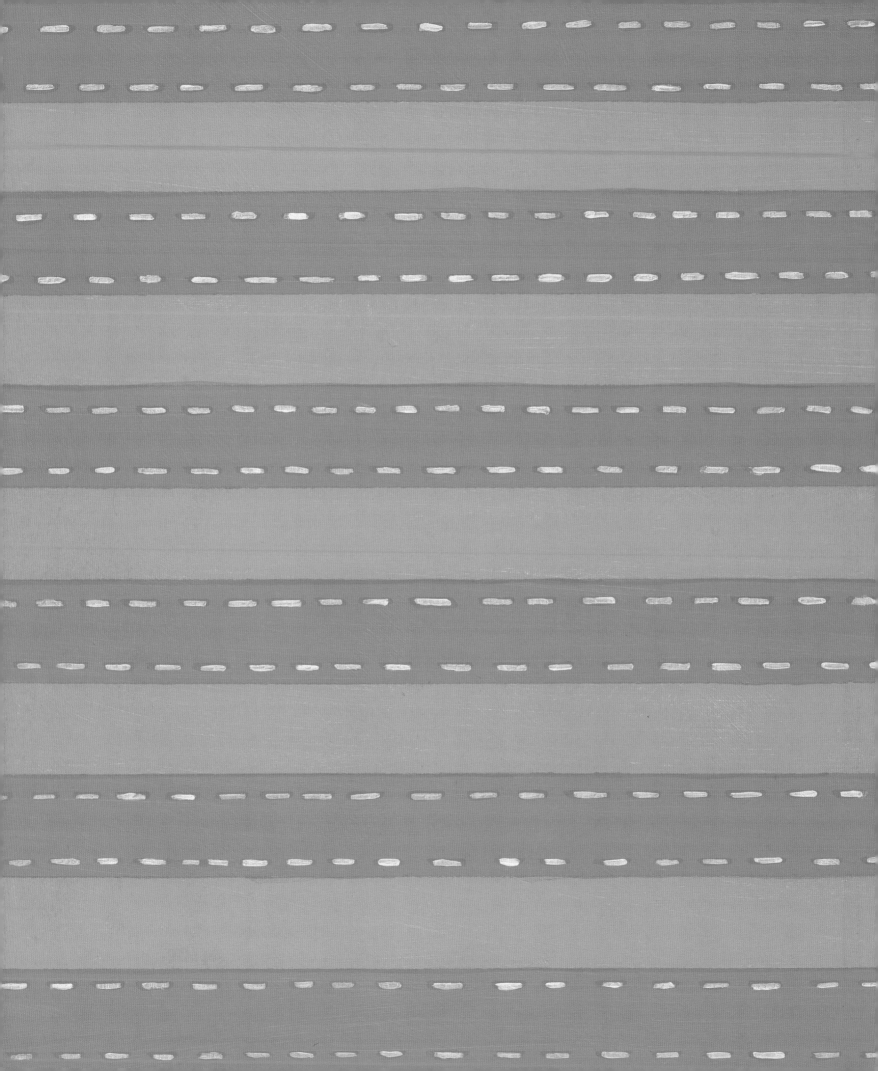